If an ELEPHANT Went to SCHOOL

ELLEN FISCHER

If an ELEPHANT Went to SCHOOL

Illustrations by
LAURA WOOD

mighty media KIDS
MINNEAPOLIS, MINNESOTA

Published by Mighty Media Kids, an imprint of Mighty Media Press, a division of Mighty Media, Inc.

This book is a work of fiction. Names, characters, places, events, and incidents are either a product of the author's imagination or are used fictitiously. Any resemblance to reality is entirely coincidental.

Library of Congress Cataloging-in-Publication Data

Fischer, Ellen, 1947-

If an elephant went to school Ellen Fischer ; illustrations by Laura Wood. -- First edition.

pages cm

ISBN 978-1-938063-61-9 (hardback) --
ISBN 978-1-938063-62-6 (ebook)

1. Animals--Habits and behavior--Fiction. 2. Schools--Fiction. 3. Learning--Fiction. 4. Humorous stories. I. Wood, Laura, 1985- illustrator. II. Title.

PZ7.F498766Ih 2015

E --dc23

2015011417

Art direction and book design by Anders Hanson, Mighty Media, Inc.

Printed and manufactured in the United States

North Mankato, Minnesota

Distributed by Publishers Group West

First edition

10 9 8 7 6 5 4 3 2 1

ELLEN FISCHER grew up in St. Louis, Missouri, but has lived in North Carolina for over thirty years. She loves to teach and write for children. She has taught elementary-age children for over twenty years and is the mother of three. She is also the author of *If an Armadillo Went to a Restaurant.*

LAURA WOOD is an illustrator currently living in England. She has a passion for catlike animals, flat shoes, and good food. When she is not busy making pictures, she drinks tea, watches movies, and spends time with the people she loves, She is also the illustrator of *If an Armadillo Went to a Restaurant.*

Dedicated with Love

to **EZRA, WILL, AND MIRIAM**

- E.L.F.

If an ELEPHANT went to school, what would she learn?

The ABCs?

NO WAY!

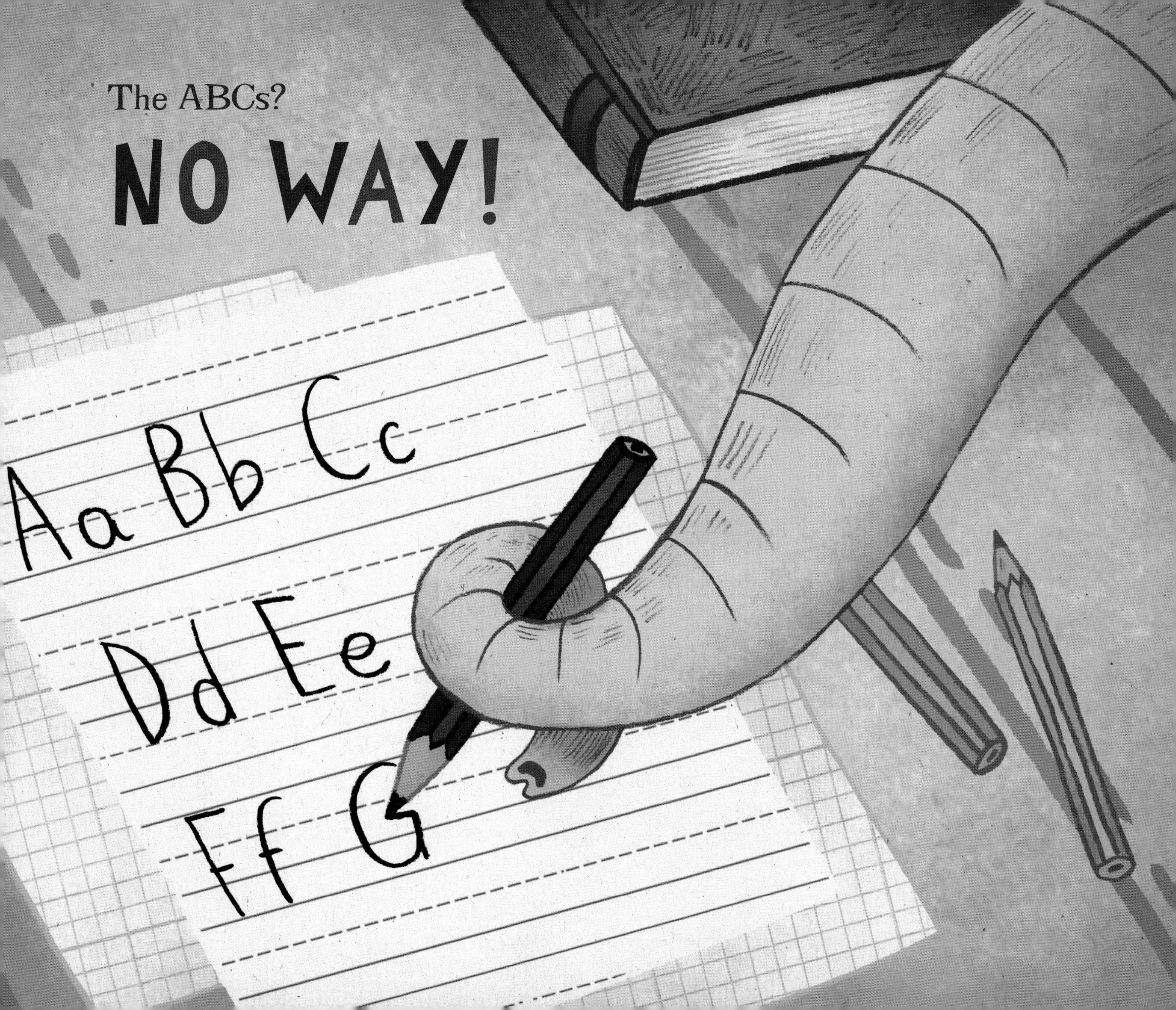

An elephant would learn to use her trunk as ...

A NOSE,

A STRAW,

A HAND, and A HOSE!

If an OWL flew to class, what would he learn?

How to count to one hundred?

I DON'T THINK SO.

An owl would learn to clean and groom his feathers with his beak.

WHO NEEDS SOAP?

If a **ZEBRA** trotted into a schoolroom, what would he learn?

FRIDAY ... AND SATURDAY!
The days of the week?
DOUBTFUL.
A zebra would learn
how to sleep standing up.
Z
Z
WITHOUT A PILLOW!

If a **FROG** hopped onto a desk, what would she learn?

How to write her name?

NOT VERY LIKELY.

A frog would
learn how to
use her tongue
to catch bugs.

ZAP!

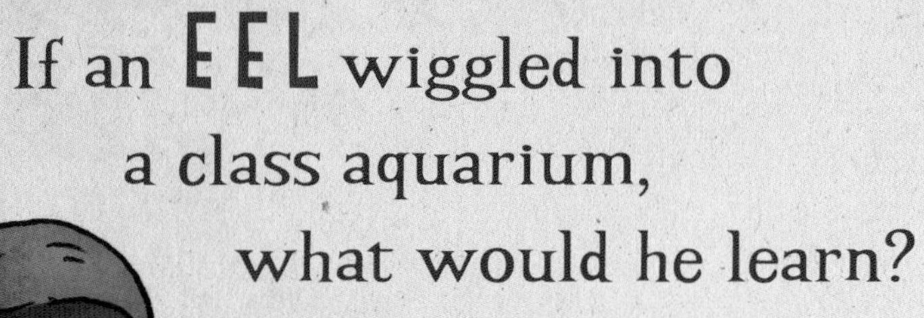

If an **EEL** wiggled into
a class aquarium,
what would he learn?

How to
skip rope?

YEAH, RIGHT!

An eel would learn
to swim backward.
NOTHING TO IT!

If a **BEE** buzzed into a school, what would she learn?

How to read?

NO, SIR!

A bee would learn
how to make honey.

YUM!

If a **SKUNK** scampered into a classroom, what would he learn?

How to build with blocks?

SURELY NOT.

A skunk would learn to use his stinky spray to stay safe.
KEEP AWAY!

If a **CATERPILLAR** crawled into a school, what would she learn?

How to write numbers?

IMPOSSIBLE!

A caterpillar would learn how to spin a cocoon.
DO NOT DISTURB.

If a **PLATYPUS** waddled into class, what would she learn?

How to play an instrument?

A platypus would learn
to dive to find her food.

NO SNORKEL NECESSARY.

If I went to school, what would I learn?

How to change colors like a chameleon?

NO
WAY!

I would learn to ...

READ,

WRITE,

SHARE, and MAKE FRIENDS.

What would **YOU** learn?